The Crane Maiden

By MIYOKO MATSUTANI

Illustrated by CHIHIRO IWASAKI

English version by ALVIN TRESSELT

This book translated from *Tsuru No Ongaeshi*
originally published by Kaisei Sha, Tokyo, Japan.

Library of Congress Catalog Card Number: 68-13357

*

PARENTS' MAGAZINE PRESS · NEW YORK

Long years ago, at the edge of a small
mountain village in the snow country
of Japan, there lived an old man
and his wife. They had little
in this world that they could call
their own, but they were happy
in their life together.

Now one winter morning the old man
set out for the village, with a bundle
of firewood fastened to his back.
It was bitter cold, and he knew
he would have little trouble selling
the wood. Then with the money, he would
buy some food so that he and his wife
could have a good supper.

As the old man trudged through the falling snow,
he was suddenly aware of a fluttering sound,
and a pitiful cry of *Koh, koh.*
Turning from the path to investigate,
he came upon a great crane
frantically trying to free herself from a trap.

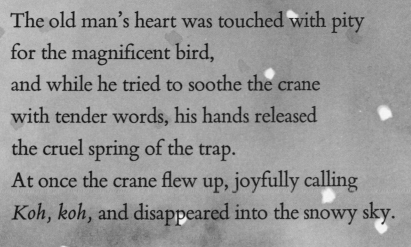

The old man's heart was touched with pity
for the magnificent bird,
and while he tried to soothe the crane
with tender words, his hands released
the cruel spring of the trap.
At once the crane flew up, joyfully calling
Koh, koh, and disappeared into the snowy sky.

With a lighter step the old man went on
through the snow, and when he had sold his wood
he returned once more to his humble house.
While his old wife busied herself
with preparing supper, he told her
about rescuing the crane.
"That was a good deed," she said.
"Surely the gods will one day
reward you for your kind heart."
As she spoke these words there came
a tapping on the door. The old wife
hastened to see who was there,
and upon opening the door, beheld
a beautiful young girl standing
in the swirling snow. Her delicate face
glowed like a peach beginning to ripen
in the summer sun, and her dark eyes
sparkled in the dancing firelight from the hearth.
          "Forgive my knocking at your door,"
          she said in a soft voice, "but
          I have lost my way in the snow.
          May I share the warmth
          of your fire tonight?"
          Then bowing low before the
          two old people, she said,
          "My name is Tsuru-san."

"Oh, you poor child!" cried the old wife.
"Come in at once before you freeze
in the bitter cold." They sat the girl down
close to the hearth, and the old wife
piled more wood on the flames so that
the girl would soon be warm.

The old couple shared their simple supper of hot porridge
with Tsuru-san, all the time feasting their eyes on her great beauty.
Then they gave her their bed with its warm quilts to sleep on,
while they spent the night huddled on a pile of straw.

In the morning when they awoke, the old man and his wife
were surprised to see a good fire already burning
on the hearth. The water urn was filled with fresh
clear water, the floors had been swept, and all the rooms
were clean and tidy.

Tsuru-san, the sleeves of her kimono neatly
tied back with a red cord, was busily stirring a pot
over the fire. "Good morning," she said, bowing
to the old couple. "If you will wash your hands
we may eat breakfast, for the porridge is cooked and ready."
"In our old age we have a daughter!" said the old man, laughing.
"It is the gods smiling on us for your good deed
of yesterday," replied his wife happily.

The snow and bitter cold continued for many days,
and so Tsuru-san stayed in the shelter of the old couple's
home. As she had neither mother nor father,
it was at last decided that she would remain
as a daughter to these people.

The children of the neighborhood were soon attracted
to the house as the girl was such a delight to be with.
The house rang with happy laughter, and the hearts
of the old man and his wife were filled with joy at the sound.

And so the days of early winter
passed, and soon it would be time
for the great New Year celebration.
The old man spoke to his wife, saying,
"Tsuru-san has been such a delight
to us. If only I could give her
a gift of a new kimono."
"Or if I could make her a rice cake
for the New Year," his wife added.
But, alas, the winter had been hard.
The old man had not been able
to cut wood to sell, so there was no money
to buy even rice, much less a kimono.
Now Tsuru-san had overheard them talking,
and it grieved her that these good people
should be so poor. Coming before
them she bowed low and said,
"Dear parents, I know there has been
no wood to sell, but perhaps I can
help you and repay your great kindness
to me. There is an old loom in the
back room. I will weave cloth on it
for you to sell in the village.
Only you must promise that no one
shall look at me while I am weaving."
The old man and his wife thought this was
an odd request, but they readily agreed.

Tsuru-san locked herself in the room,
and soon they heard the sound of
Tin kola, kola, pon, pon,
Tin kola, kola, pon, pon—
as the shuttle sped back and forth
and the fabric grew in length.

For three days this continued, and Tsuru-san
paused for neither food nor rest. Then at last
the door opened and she stepped out, holding
in her hands a bolt of cloth
such as the old man and his
wife had never seen in all
their lives. They gasped
at its beauty, and marveled
at its incredible softness.
"Dear father," said the girl,
"take this cloth into the village
and sell it. It will be but small
payment for the happy home you
have given me. Remember this,
however," she continued. "Do not
put a price on this cloth, and you
will fare better than you can imagine."

Without wasting a moment, the old man hurried into the center of the village, and when people saw the beautiful cloth he was carrying, a crowd soon gathered.

"I will pay ten gold pieces for your cloth," said one man.

"No, no!" cried another. "Sell it to me for twenty gold pieces!"

"You would be a fool to sell it for such a price, old man,"
said another. "This is a bolt of rare twilled brocade.
I will pay you fifty gold pieces for it." And so it went,
with each man offering more, until the old man finally
sold the cloth for one hundred pieces of gold.

Pausing only long enough to buy
rice for rice cakes, a kimono for
Tsuru-san and a few delicacies
for New Year's Day, the man
hurried home with his pockets
jingling. "Tomorrow, tomorrow
is the New Year's Day," he sang.
"The New Year is the happy time,
eating rice cakes whiter than snow,
drinking sake that is smoother
than oil."

Then such a hustle and bustle
there was, as the old man and
his wife prepared for the feast.
As he pounded the rice, his wife
made it into fine white cakes.
And on New Year's Day all the
children came in for a great party
with their friend, Tsuru-san.

Still the cold days of winter followed one after the other,
until at last one day Tsuru-san said to the old couple,
"It is time for me to weave another bolt of cloth
for you so that you will have money to live until the
spring returns. But remember what I told you. No one
is to look at me while I am working."
Again they promised that they would not, and the girl
once more locked herself in the room and began weaving.

Tin kola, kola, pon, pon,
Tin kola, pon, pon—
went the loom.
One day passed, and then the second.
Still the sound of the loom
filled the house. By now,
the neighbors had grown curious.

"Is·Tsuru–san weaving again?"
asked one.
"Ah, soon you will have more gold
pieces to hide under the floor,"
said another with a smile and a wink.
"The loom makes such an interesting
sound," remarked the first one.
"I would love to see
what Tsuru–san is doing."

"We have promised not to watch her while she works,"
said the old man.

"What an odd request," cried one of the people.

"I would not make such a promise to *my* daughter,
you can believe me. What harm could there be
in taking one look?"

Now in truth, the old woman had been most curious
about Tsuru-san's weaving, and encouraged
by her neighbor's remarks,
she stepped up to a crack
in the door.

"Stop, stop, old woman!" cried her husband when he saw what was happening. "Tsuru-san has forbidden it!" But it was too late. His wife had already peeked through the crack.

What a sight it was that met her eye!
There, sitting at the loom, was a great white crane,
pulling feathers from her body
and miraculously weaving them into cloth.

The old woman stepped back from the door, and before
she could relate what she had seen, the door opened.
Out stepped Tsuru-san, thin and pale, holding in her
hands a half-finished bolt of cloth. "Dear parents,"
she said in a weak voice, "I am the crane you rescued
from the trap. I wanted to repay your kindness by weaving
you another bolt of cloth." Then her eyes filled with tears.
"But now that you have seen me in my true form
I can no longer stay with you."

With this she kissed the man and his wife tenderly,
and walked out of the house. Instantly she became
a crane once more, and with a great whish of her wings
flew up into the sky. Slowly she circled overhead,
then with a single cry of *Koh* as if to say good-bye,
the crane maiden was gone forever.